MW00955221

MIA ROY
Learns to Share
Story by
Herbenesha Smith

Bird House Publishing
A Bird House Enterprises LLC Company
8325 Broadway Street, Ste. 202 |Pearland, TX 77581 | (832) 535-2362
Bird House Publishing is committed to filling the need for more diverse books. We are also committed to the relentless pursuit of equity, authenticity, and inclusion. We encourage all of our readers and authors to show up in the world as their best selves. Our stories build empathy, coping skills, courage, and curiosity to explore cultures other than our own.
We are always looking for diverse and thoughtful voices to share with the world.

ISBN: 978-1-7343217-6-0

Bird House Publishing rev date 06/28/21

To my mother. There is an old African proverb that says "it takes a village to raise a child." Mom, you are an entire village unto yourself. The sacrifices that you have made for us cannot be repaid. You propel me forward and I love you.

The weekend is here! MiaRoy and mommy are packed up and on their way to grandma's house. It's "cousins" weekend.

¡Llegó el fin de semana! MiaRoy y mamá empacan y se dirigen a la casa de la abuela. Es el fin de semana de "primos".

MiaRoy bursts through grandma's door with excitement and greets everyone with hugs and kisses. MiaRoy notices her baby cousin, Reesie, playing with her doll that she left behind the last time she came to visit grandma.
MiaRoy irrumpe por la puerta de la abuela con emoción y saluda a todos con abrazos y besos. MiaRoy se da cuenta de su prima menor, Reesie, juega con su muñeca que dejó la última vez que vino a visitar a la abuela.

MiaRoy snatches the doll from Reesie, and yells, "It's mine!" Reesie begins to cry.

MiaRoy le quita la muñeca a Reesie y grita, "¡Es mía!" Reesie comienza a llorar.

Now MiaRoy has her doll, but she notices her big cousins, L.C. and Austin, playing with one of her favorite stuffed animals, Dimo the dinosaur. “Oh no,” says MiaRoy!

Ahora MiaRoy tiene su muñeca, pero se da cuenta de que sus primos mayores, L.C. y Austin, jugando con uno de sus peluches favoritos, Dimo el dinosaurio. “¡Oh, no,” dice Mia!

MiaRoy rushes over yelling,
"That's my Dimo!"

MiaRoy corre gritando,
"¡Ese es mi Dimo!"

A tug-of-war begins between the three cousins.

Comienza un tira y afloja entre los tres primos.

MiaRoy yells, “It’s mine,” and snatches Dimo away.

MiaRoy grita, “Es mío” y se lleva a Dimo.

MiaRoy walks away with both of her toys tucked under her arms and a grin of contentment across her face.

MiaRoy se aleja con sus dos juguetes debajo de los brazos y una sonrisa de contenido en su cara.

Later that evening, MiaRoy spots her cousins playing in a big circle. She calls out to them, "Hey guys, wait for me!"

Más tarde esa noche, MiaRoy ve a sus primos jugando en un gran círculo. Ella les grita, "¡Hola primos espérenme!"

As MiaRoy approaches
the circle, Reesie yells,
"I don't want to play with her!
She took dolly!" L.C.
and Austin yell, "Me neither!
She took Dimo from us!"

Cuando MiaRoy se acerca
al círculo, Reesie grita,
"¡No quiero jugar con ella!
¡Se llevó la muñeca!" L.C. y
Austin grita, "¡Nos tampoco!
¡Nos quitó a Dimo!"

MiaRoy walks away crying.

MiaRoy se va llorando.

Mommy spots MiaRoy playing by herself with a sad face and asks, “What’s wrong, baby girl?” MiaRoy replies, “My cousins don’t want to play with me because I didn’t want to share my dolly and Dimo.”

Mommy replies, “I’m sure your cousins don’t mind playing with you. Maybe their feelings are hurt because you didn’t share your toys. Sharing with family and friends is a way to express our love. You should give it a try.”

Mamá ve a MiaRoy jugando sola con una cara triste y pregunta, “¿Qué pasa, niña?” MiaRoy responde, “Mis primos no quieren jugar conmigo porque no quería compartir mi muñeca y Dimo”.

Mamá responde, “Estoy segura de que a tus primos les encantaría jugar contigo. Es posible que sus sentimientos se sientan heridos porque no compartiste tus juguetes. Compartir con familia y amigos es una forma de expresar nuestro amor. Deberías probarlo.”

MiaRoy approaches her cousins again, bringing along dolly and Dimo. She says, "I'm sorry. You all can play with Dimo and dolly." The cousins give MiaRoy a big group hug and invite her to play in their circle.

MiaRoy vuelve a acercarse a sus primos, trayendo a Dolly y Dimo. Ella dice, "Lo siento. Todos pueden jugar con Dimo y Dolly". Los primos le dan a MiaRoya un gran abrazo grupal y la invitan a jugar en su círculo.

FINISH

Used My
Manners

Techniques to Encourage Sharing

Técnicas para fomentar el intercambio

1. Praise positive behavior. This is the time to show your child how happy and excited you are to see them doing a great job of sharing.
2. Compliment their behavior!
3. Role play with your child to show them how you would like them to behave when sharing.
4. Give rewards! Small items, such as stickers, or allowing the child to take part in their favorite activities is rewarding.
5. If the child has a sibling or playmate, use a timer to allow the kids to take turns sharing a toy or item.
6. Don't force it! Learning social skills is not an overnight process. It takes time!
7. Repeat the above steps weekly, and, eventually, the child will learn.

1. Celebrar el comportamiento positivo. Este es el momento de mostrarle a su hijo lo feliz y emocionado que se siente al verlos haciendo un gran trabajo al compartir.
2. ¡Dale cumplidos a su comportamiento!
3. Haga un juego de roles con su hijo para mostrarle cómo le gustaría que se comportara al compartir.
4. Da recompensas! Los artículos pequeños, como pegatinas, o permitir su niño participe en sus actividades favoritas.
5. Si el niño tiene un hermano o un compañero de juegos, use un temporizador para permitir que los niños se turnen para compartir los juguetes.
6. No lo fuerces! El aprendizaje de habilidades sociales no es un proceso que pueda apresurarse. ¡Toma tiempo!
7. Repita los pasos anteriores semanalmente y, eventualmente, el niño aprenderá.

CPSIA information can be obtained
at www.ICGtesting.com
Printed in the USA
BVHW021133270122
627375BV00002B/31

* 9 7 8 1 7 3 4 3 2 1 7 6 0 *